Father Abraham

BY

William Faulkner

EDITED BY James B. Meriwether
WITH WOOD ENGRAVINGS BY John DePol

Random House New York

Library of Congress Cataloging in Publication Data
Faulkner, William, 1897-1962.
Father Abraham.
I. Title.
PS3511.A86F37   1984   813'.54   83-43204
ISBN 0-394-53722-x

Manufactured in the United States of America
9 8 7 6 5 4 3 2
First Edition

The original limited edition was
designed by Ken Botnick and Steve Miller and produced
at the Red Ozier Press in New York. The text type is
Emerson, cast at Out of Sorts Letter Foundery,
& the title page calligraphy is by Anita Karl.

INTRODUCTION

Not a fragment, not quite a finished work, *Father Abraham* is the brilliant beginning of a novel which William Faulkner tried repeatedly to write, for a period of almost a decade and a half, during the earlier part of his career—the novel about the Snopes family which he finally completed and published as *The Hamlet* in 1940.

The twenty-four-page manuscript of *Father Abraham* here first published is apparently the earliest surviving attempt at this Snopes novel. Probably written late in 1926, by early 1927 it had been abandoned for another novel, *Flags in the Dust*, which Faulkner went on to complete later that year, and which was published in a much-edited and cut-down version, entitled *Sartoris*, in 1929.

But the unfinished Snopes novel continued to plague him. He made further efforts to write it in the late 1920's and early 1930's, trying different titles ('Abraham's Children,' 'The Peasants'), making short stories out of episodes he had planned or drafted for the novel ('Centaur in Brass,' 'Wash'), even making large parts of entire novels, like *As I Lay Dying* and *Absalom, Absalom!*, out of the ideas and materials that had originally belonged to the Snopes book. When he finished writing *The Hamlet*, one of his longest novels, he still had so much material remaining that he planned at least two more books about the Snopeses, though it was not till late in his career that he finally got around to writing *The Town* (1957) and *The Mansion* (1959). And in 1964, two years after his death, all three volumes of the trilogy were brought out together, as he had wished, with the title *Snopes*.

Father Abraham, then, marks the inception of a work that altogether spans nearly the whole of Faulkner's career as a writer of fiction, a work that includes some of his best writing and which, as it evolved, had profound effects upon much of the rest of it. After *Father Abraham*, no matter what other novels and stories he turned to, Faulkner's Snopeses would be a vital part of what he called the 'lumber room' of his imagination, and the completion of their saga would be one of his major ambitions—or obligations—as an artist.

Why, then, did he for so long leave *Father Abraham*

unfinished—at least as a novel? Surely he felt no dissatisfaction with what he had already written—the introduction of Flem Snopes and his tribe, and the magnificent tale of the auction of the wild Texas range ponies which he used in his 1931 short story 'Spotted Horses,' and so much of which he carried over directly into *The Hamlet*, almost a decade later. But changes in his original conception of the Snopeses, and the need to expand the scope as well as the size of their book, obviously caused Faulkner problems which he had great difficulty in resolving.

One problem may have been the need to outgrow an influence, or at least to achieve a certain amount of distance from it. All three volumes of the trilogy were dedicated by Faulkner to his early friend and mentor Phil Stone, a lawyer and fellow-townsman in Oxford, Mississippi with whom, in the 1920's, he worked up many of the characters and incidents that eventually went into *The Hamlet* and *The Town*. Though the two friends parted ways later on, at the beginning of Faulkner's career they were very close, and it is clear that Stone's ideas were still important to Faulkner at the time *Father Abraham* was begun.

In a 1957 letter, Stone recalled that the idea for the Snopeses, and their book, had been his, and that he had given it to Faulkner after *Mosquitoes* (his second novel, published in April 1927) was written but before the writing of *Sartoris*. 'The core of the Snopes legend,' explained Stone, was 'that the real revolution in the South was not the race situation but the rise of the redneck, who did not have any of the scruples of the old aristocracy, to places of power and wealth.' And he recalled that 'Bill once wrote fifteen or twenty pages on the idea of the Snopes trilogy which he entitled 'Father Abraham' but I think that has disappeared.' Stone's recollection seems accurate, both for the date and for his own attitude, at least, towards the lowly origins of the Snopeses. In a piece he wrote early in 1927, for the local paper, announcing the forthcoming publication of *Mosquitoes*, he mentioned a Faulkner novel in progress which, he said, 'is something of a saga of an extensive family connection of typical "poor white trash" and is said by those who have seen that part of the manuscript completed to be the funniest book anybody ever wrote.'

At the time he wrote *Father Abraham*, Faulkner's attitude

towards the Snopeses was very near to Stone's, and he probably shared to some extent Stone's aristocratic condescension towards 'rednecks' and 'poor white trash.' But the creator of Will Varner and V. K. Suratt, or even of Eck Snopes, already possessed a much broader, more sympathetic view of human nature and society than did Stone, and in order to go on from *Father Abraham* to *The Hamlet*, Faulkner had to go far beyond the friend who had originally contributed so much to the idea of the Snopeses and their book.

Behind the immediate influence of Phil Stone's ideas, and the Snopeslore the two men invented in yarnspinning sessions, lay a wealth of experience and reading Faulkner could draw on in creating the Snopeses and their neighbors and their book. In the memoir of Faulkner that his brother John wrote, he recalled an occasion (Faulkner's biographer, Joseph Blotner, assigns it the date 1922) when William was helping their Uncle John Falkner, Jr. in his campaign for a District Court judgeship.

Bill was sitting on the front porch of the boardinghouse late that evening when some men brought in a string of calico ponies wired together with barbed wire. They put them in a lot just across the road from the boardinghouse and the next morning auctioned them off, at prices ranging from about five dollars apiece on up.

Just like in Bill's story, the men sold all the horses, put the money in their pockets and left. When the buyers went in to get their purchases, someone left the gate open and those ponies spread like colored confetti over the countryside.

Bill sat there on the porch of the boardinghouse and saw it all. One of them ran the length of the porch and he had to dive back into the hallway to get out of its path. He and Uncle John told us about it the next day, when they got home.

To such raw material Faulkner would soon be able to bring the literary skills he needed to make it into the substance of *Father Abraham*, into his own highly individual blend of realism and comedy—comedy constantly threatening to turn into tragedy and always inclining towards myth. In New Orleans, in 1925, Faulkner came to know Sherwood Anderson, whose *Winesburg,*

Ohio and *Horses and Men* the younger writer particularly admired, and with whom he invented tall tales of the Al Jackson family, descended from Andrew Jackson and 'no longer half-horse half-alligator but by now half-man half-sheep and presently half-shark,' as Faulkner recalled in 1953. Some of the Al Jackson material made its way into *Mosquitoes* and its influence upon the conception of the Snopeses is obvious. Earlier literary antecedents abounded, in an earlier America, especially in the South. In Constance Rourke's *American Humor* she describes such material and what was done with it by other writers:

> Scalawags, gamblers, n'er-do-wells, small rapscallions, or mere corncrackers were drawn into a careless net of stories, against a background of pine-barrens, sandy wastes, half-plowed fields, huts with leaky roofs. Their implements were rusty, their houses wall-eyed and spavined. They be-longed to a rootless drift that had followed in the wake of huntsmen and scout, and they were not wholly different in kind. Sly instead of strong, they pursued uncharted ways, breaking from traditions, bent on triumph. . . . [The center of these stories was] Grotesquerie and irreverence and upset . . . caricature was drawn in a single line or phrase. 'He drawed in the puckerin'-string ov that legil face of his'n,' said Sut Lovingood of a sheriff.

We might recall that Faulkner knew and admired the book from which she quotes that description — George Washington Harris's *Sut Lovingood Yarns* (1867), and the description itself recalls *Father Abraham's* I. O. Snopes, with 'his mean little features clotted in the middle of his face like the plucking gesture of a hand.'

Obviously Faulkner is writing of the plain people of the rural South, in *Father Abraham*, consciously within the tradition of Harris, and of A. B. Longstreet and Mark Twain, with their humor of exaggeration, their unsentimental view of human nature, and their celebration of the literary possibilities of the American vernacular. And he enjoys showing the vitality of that oral tradition when his character V. K. Suratt, the sewing machine salesman, 'with the studied effectiveness of the professional humorist,' converts the raw material of the experience he has just had into an artfully woven narrative for his audience on the veranda of Will Varner's country store. Suratt (renamed Ratliff in *The Hamlet*) was to become one of Faulkner's favorite characters; though he comes from much the same background, he is the natural antagonist of the cold and silent and humorless Flem Snopes.

The title of the work is ironic, and it is to Flem that it refers. The explanation appears not in *Father Abraham* but in *Flags in the Dust*, where Flem's arrival in Jefferson is described:

> Flem, the first Snopes, had appeared unheralded one day and without making a ripple in the town's life, behind the counter of a small restaurant on a side street, patronized by country people. With this foothold and like Abraham of old, he led his family piece by piece into town.

Only in later works does Faulkner make Flem's impotence certain; but even here it is apparent that there is a monstrous irony in the comparison with the Old Testament Abraham, father of many, founder of Judaism. Flem, the worshipper of money, may be leader of a clan, but he is father to no one.

Father Abraham is perhaps a little unpolished, a little awkward, in places. The opening description of Flem, already in town, in his bank, unjealous of his wife, already both Snopes and symbol of Snopesism, is a little stilted compared to the easy and relaxed narration of the following flashback to his origins in Frenchman's Bend. The last sentence dangles—it is a temptation to omit it and end the work with that final surrealistic vision of twilight and evening in Frenchman's Bend, into which Faulkner brings so many tags and images from the poetry he had been writing, and into which he brings the reader with a striking departure from the hard-edged realism and rich vernacular humor of the main body of the story. But its flaws are minor compared with its accomplishment. The young Faulkner—that is, the writer he was until he wrote *The Sound and the Fury*—did nothing more ambitious, or more successful.

James B. Meriwether

A NOTE ON THE TEXT

This edition reproduces, with a minimum of editorial alteration, the text of the twenty-four page holograph manuscript in the Arents Collection of the New York Public Library. It is written on legal-sized sheets, numbered 1 through 25, with page 23 missing. The handwriting is not, in general, difficult to read, but there are a few passages where haste or the need to save space made Faulkner's usually precise if tiny letters almost illegible. In deciphering these I have not hesitated to consult various later manuscript and typescript versions of the work; however, I have resisted the temptation to use them as authority to emend or revise this text, even though a closely-related later version of a passage may smooth out awkwardnesses in grammar or punctuation.

Some changes were necessary, however, in preparing a reading text from a manuscript that was never intended by its author to go to the printer. In preparing typescript printer's copy from a manuscript Faulkner always made certain changes which I have adopted here: making new paragraphs by indention instead of by extra spacing, expanding various abbreviations, adding necessary punctuation to new material inserted in the margins, converting arabic numerals to words. A few slips of the pen have been corrected, a few quotation marks have been added, and a few proper and place names have been made consistent—e.g., Frenchman's bend and Frenchman's Bend. However, I have left unaltered such consistent, if idiosyncratic, Faulkner practices as the omitted apostrophes from one-syllable contractions like dont and cant, the omitted periods after Mr and Mrs; and I have left unmodernized certain habitual spellings, like rythm and whip-porwill, which lead to no confusion and have adequate historical justification. In trying to steer a middle course between a more literal transcription of the manuscript, which would have pleased scholars, and a more modernized, regularized, and corrected version, which might have made smoother going for the general reader, I have had to make compromises; but I hope the final result is a text appropriate both to this particular work and to the audience for which it was written.

J. B. M.

FATHER ABRAHAM

He is a living example
of the astonishing byblows of man's utopian dreams
actually functioning; in this case the dream is Demo-
cracy. He will become legendary in time, but he has
always been symbolic. Legendary as Roland and as
symbolic of a form of behavior; as symbolic of an age
and a region as his predecessor, a portly man with a
white imperial and a shoestring tie and a two gallon
hat, was; as symbolic and as typical of a frame of mind
as Buddha is today. With this difference: Buddha
contemplates an abstraction and derives a secret amuse-
ment of it; while he behind the new plate glass window
of his recently remodelled bank, dwells with neither
lust nor alarm on the plump yet still disturbing image
of his silkclad wife passing the time of day with
Colonel Winword in front of the postoffice.

Thus he comes into the picture, thus he goes out of
it, ruminant and unwinking and timeless. As Buddha,
through a blending of successive avatars, was in the
beginning Complete and will be Complete when
thought has long since progressed logically into a frigid
region without sight nor sound where amid sunless
space the I become a sightless eye contemplates itself
in timeless unsurprise, so with him. What boots it that

13

for many years his corporeal illusion was not so smugly
flourishing, that for many years he was too busy to sit
down and, when he did, looked not out upon the world
through plate glass? Buddha had his priests to invent a
cult for him while he stirred not a finger; while he must
be god cult priest and ritual simultaneously; Buddha
drew followers by mouthsounds, he bought them with
the very blood in his veins. This, behind its plate glass,
its quiet unwinking eyes, its mouth like one of those
patent tobacco pouches you open and close by ripping
a metal ring along the seam, this is the man. It boots not
that for thirty years the town itself saw him not four
times a year, that for the next fifteen years the bank
knew him only on the customer's side of the savings'
window; this was, is and will be, the man. The Lord
said once to Moses: "I am that I am" and Moses argued
with the good God; but when he spoke to one of his
chosen, that one replied immediately: "Here am I,
Uncle Flem." He chews tobacco constantly and steadily
and slowly, and no one ever saw his eyelids closed. He
blinks them of course, like everybody else, but no one
ever saw him do it. This is the man.

The story first finds him where the light of day
found him. Twenty miles southeast of Jefferson, in the
hill cradled cane and cypress jungles of Yocona river
lies the settlement of Frenchman's Bend. To the urban
southerner anyone who speaks the language with a
foreign flavor or whose appearance or occupation is
strange, is a dutchman. His rural brother though, being either more catholic or more of a precisian, calls
the outlander a frenchman. The original settler of
Frenchman's Bend could easily have been Louisiana

French, however, but this is not known. He is gone, with his family and his splendor. His broad acres are parcelled out in small shiftless farms which the jungle is taking again, and all that remains of him is the river-bed which he straightened out to keep his land from overflowing in the spring and the skeleton of a huge colonial house which neighbors have been pulling down piecemeal for fifty years and burning it a plank at a time for firewood, amid its grove of oaks.

But the Frenchman himself is forgotten, and his pride is now but a legend upon the land he had wrested from the earth and tamed and made fruitful: a monument to himself against the time when sleep should come upon his eyelids and depart not from them again; a legend which no longer has anything to do with the man even. The man is gone, his dream and his pride are dust with the lost dust of his anonymous bones, and in its place but the stubborn legend of the gold he buried when Grant swept through the land on his way to Chickamauga.

The inhabitants of Frenchman's Bend are of Scottish and Irish and English blood. There are Turpins here, and Haleys and Whittingtons, and McCallums and Murrays and Leonards and Littlejohns; and other family names which only the good God himself could have invented—sound peasant names from the midlands and the Scottish and Welsh marches, which have passed from mouth to mouth after the generations had forgotten how to read and spell—Starnes and Snopes and Quick—ridiculous names until you remember that the soil had bred them long ago and the soil has nourished them down the untarnished ages until their

15

owners have come to accept them at the true value of
a name: a sound by which a man may be singled from
a crowd. Let the city fools alter and corrupt and prune
and graft their appellations to fit euphony or fashion if
they will. They till the soil in the cleared bottom land
and grow cotton on it, and till the soil along the edge
of the hills and raise corn on it, and in the second growth
pine clad hills they make whiskey out of the corn and
sell what they do not drink. County officers do not
annoy them save at election time, and they support
their own churches and schools, and sow the land and
reap it and kill each other occasionally and commit
adultery and fear God and hate republicans and niggers.

Uncle Billy Varner is the big man of the Frenchman's Bend neighborhood. Beat supervisor, politician,
farmer, usurer, present owner of the dead Frenchman's
homestead and the legend. Uncle Billy is a tall reddish
colored man with little bright blue eyes: he looks like a
Methodist elder, and is; and a milder mannered man
never foreclosed a mortgage or carried a voting precinct.
He wears a turnip shaped silver watch on a plaited
horsehair chain and his son in law is election commis-
sioner for the precinct and his son owns the store and is
postmaster of Frenchman's Bend. The rest of Uncle
Billy's family consists of a gray placid wife and a daugh-
ter of sixteen or so—a softly ample girl with eyes like
cloudy hothouse grapes and a mouth always slightly
open in a kind of moist unalarmed surprise and a body
that, between rare and reluctant movements, falls into
attitudes passively and richly disturbing to the male
beholder.

And quite a few of them come to behold. The young

16

men from the surrounding countryside gather like
wasps about the placid honey of her being; they ride
in to church on Sunday morning and linger about the
shadespotted portals until Uncle Billy drives up in his
surrey, his wife beside him and Eula and her chosen
swain stiffly arrayed and garnished on the back seat;
and always one saddle or driving horse and often three
or four doze and stamp the long Sunday afternoons
away beneath the oaks before Uncle Billy's house while
their owners uncomfortable in Sunday finery perch
stiff and fuming on Uncle Billy's veranda, doggedly
sitting each other out. So the afternoon passes. Eula
rife and richly supine in the porch swing, showing
no partiality; and the afternoon falls into a drowse of
heat and the odor of Eula's washed and scented flesh
is terribly sweet to the young men with a week of
manual labor behind them and another week waiting
on the morrow. So they sit leashed and savage and
loud amid her rich responsive giggles until the shadows
merge eastward and night falls upon the land and
the crickets raise their dry monotonous voices from
the dew, and the frogs quaver and thump from the
creekside and whipporwills are quiring among the
trees and the cold remains of dinner have been eaten
beneath the moth swirled lamp. Then the young
men give up and depart in a body and ride in seething
and wordless amity to the ford across the creek half
a mile away, where they get down and hitch their
horses and fight silently and viciously and remount
their horses and take their separate ways, temporarily
freed of jealousy and anger and thwarted desire, across
the planted land, beneath the moon.

17

Eula was a very popular girl. She attended all
the dances and picnics and meetings and allday
singings within ten miles, and with the best young
blood of the countryside she drove homeward beneath
the moon or the summer stars, along quiet roads
gashed vaguely across the dark land, behind rythmic
horses between the fecund fields and lightless houses
slumbering beside the road, and dark wood patches
feathering their tops against the stars and whipporwills like snared stars in audible bursts among the
trees or blundering out of the dust beneath the horse's
hoofs. And life would seem remote and disturbing
and exquisitely sad to them beneath the overarching
trees, and the horse's feet plopped quietly and without
haste in the sandy dust and the buggy wheels turned
through the sand with continuous secretive sounds,
and the road dropped gradually and the darkness
grew denser, with a low wet smell in it and the horse
stopped and lowered his head and snorted into the
murmurous invisible water of the ford........

One day one of the young bucks of the village sold
his new yellow wheeled runabout and his matched
horses and departed for Texas. The next day Uncle
Billy Varner and Eula and Flem Snopes, the clerk in
Uncle Billy's son's store, drove into Jefferson, the
county seat. Here Flem Snopes bought a wedding
license and he and Eula were married. Uncle Billy made
them a wedding present of forty acres of land which
included the old Frenchman's homesite, and the third
day Flem was sitting again in the door of the store,
chewing his tobacco and minding his own endless

18

affairs, as usual. The fourth day it was learned that another young man, son of a well to do farmer five or six miles down the river, had also moved to Texas.

Flem Snopes had always been a great one for attending to his own business, so much so that his employer often wondered coldly if Flem ever would tot up the column, strike a balance and close the ledger. But if Flem ever did do so, no one ever knew it, and had his employer ever learned Flem's single axiom of social relations, he would have been astonished, if not alarmed. For Flem had reduced all human conduct to a single workable belief: that some men are fools but all men are no honester than the occasion requires.

Ten years ago Flem had appeared one day behind the counter of Varner's store—a quiet unwinking slightly bowlegged young man. His eyes were all surface and were the color of stagnant water, and you never saw his eyelids closed over them, even momentarily, and his tobacco pouch seam of a mouth was slightly stained at the corners with snuff. He had brought his own secret affairs with him and at thirty he was still pursuing with a quiet implacability their devious and hidden turns. Lending money at exorbitant interest, buying and selling live stock, turning an odd penny here and there. The only concession he had made to his more sophisticated surroundings was to substitute chewing tobacco for snuff.

The Snopes sprang untarnished from a long line of shiftless tenant farmers—a race that is of the land and yet rootless, like mistletoe; owing nothing to the soil, giving nothing to it and getting nothing of it in return;

using the land as a harlot instead of an imperious yet abundant mistress, passing on to another farm. Cunning and dull and clannish, they move and halt and move and multiply and marry and multiply like rabbits: magnify them and you have political hangerson and professional officeholders and prohibition officers; reduce the perspective and you have mold on cheese, steadfast and gradual and implacable: theirs that dull provincial cunning that causes them to doubt anything that does not jibe with their preconceived and arbitrary standards of verity, and that permits them to be taken in by the most barefaced liar who is at all plausible.

Three years after Flem came to the settlement proper, a second Snopes appeared, likewise unannounced. One day he was not there, the next day he was working in the blacksmith shop; two years later he was married to a local maiden and owned the blacksmith shop, which he operated with the assistance of a third Snopes who looked exactly like him, and was to be seen on Sunday propelling a fourth Snopes in a homemade perambulator, to the Methodist church.

So Flem was not the first Snopes to wed a Frenchman's Bend belle. Though nobody had expected Flem to take a partner of any sort into that endless and secret business of his, let alone Uncle Billy Varner's Eula, who had half the yellow wheeled buggies in the vicinity tied to her fence of a Sunday while their owners shook cigar ashes over the veranda railing onto Mrs Varner's geraniums. But two of these had gone suddenly to Texas and the other yellow wheeled buggies rested the long drowsy Sunday afternoons away before other houses about the countryside, and Flem Snopes had moved his straw suitcase to Uncle Billy's house and, chewing his tobacco with a rythmic implacable thrusting of his lower jaw, he went steadily and implacably about his endless secret affairs. Occasionally he was Sunday afternoons seen chewing his tobacco about the old Frenchman's place which was his wife's marriage portion, and people believed that he was planning to build on it. But a month or so after the marriage he and his wife also moved to Texas, which is quite a large though virgin state.

II

Texas in those days was a large easy region, with boundaries in Washington, D.C. And conventional: you grew cotton, or raised cattle or stole it from those who did; and Flem Snopes, who had never put anything into the ground except a long succession of baking powder tins that rusted slowly in the quiet earth about a growing niggard hoard of coins and filthy bills, and who neither owned nor desired a pistol and who had no more use for a horse than he had for three percent interest, found Texas crude.

Eula doubtless agreed with him, for one day in early spring and about a year after her wedding, Uncle Billy Varner drove into Jefferson and returned with Eula and a bouncing granddaughter. It was a fine child, remarkably wellgrown, and Mrs Varner immediately and voluntarily became its bond slave, carrying it about the neighborhood or hovering about it with a fond raptness while it clawed itself erect from chair to chair, already evincing a desire to walk. Meanwhile Eula, altered a little by motherhood, but still rifely and placidly disturbing to the male beholder, settled down once more in Uncle Billy's home. She resigned all maternal obligations to her mother, and passed her days helping about the house and, on Sundays, in fresh print dresses she sat on the veranda while evening grew, looking placidly out across the lawn and the fence beneath the locust trees where once flashy yellow wheeled buggies had stood while the combed and curried horses that drew them stamped the long drowsy afternoons away, and beyond, down the quiet road stretching on beneath the budding trees.

Then it was April. Peach and pear and apple were in bloom, and blackbirds swung and stooped with raucous cries like rusty shutters in the wind, and like random scraps of burned paper slanted across the fields, and new fledged willow-screens beyond which waters chuckled and murmured with the grave continuous irrelevance of children, and behind surging horses and mules men broke the land anew and the turned earth smelled like new calves in a clean barn, and sowed it, and nightly the new moon waxed in the windless west and soon stood by day though incomplete in the marbled zenith. Thus the world, and on a day Flem Snopes came up the road in a covered wagon, accompanied by a soiled swaggering man in a clay colored Stetson hat and a sweeping black moustache, and followed by a score of horses larger than rabbits and colored like patchwork quilts and shackled one to another with sections of barbed wire.

"Startin' you a circus, Flem?" asked a casual in overalls, and other casuals squatting on their heels against the wall of Varner's store came to see, and Jody Varner in a white shirt and a brass collar button came out also and approached the ponies and one of the ponies stood on its hind feet and tried to beat Jody Varner's face in.

"Keep away from 'em, boys," the black moustached man said, "They've got kind of skittish, they aint been rode in so long." He descended heavily, in boots. His belly fitted like a round wedge into the tops of his corduroy pants, and from his hip pocket protruded a heavy pistol-butt and a gay pasteboard carton. "They'll settle down once they've been worked a day or so," he added.

"What you aim to do with 'em, Flem?" Jody Varner asked curiously, from a safe distance, while the pony watched him with a pale cerulean eye. But Flem Snopes only chewed his tobacco with his customary

23

rythmic thrust and climbed down on the other side
of the wagon and retreated toward the store, where
Jody Varner presently followed him.

The stranger's ear on the off side had been recently
and almost completely sheared from his head and the
severed edge of the remainder had been treated with
a blackish substance resembling axel grease. Through
the hair on the back of his neck were slashed two
vicious furrows, and he drew the cardboard carton
from his pocket and shook a gingersnap into his other
hand and inserted it beneath his moustache. The vari-
colored ponies huddled behind the wagon, wild as
rabbits, deadly as rattlesnakes, and quiet as doves.
Other casuals came up, and they stood quietly about,
looking at the ponies and the stranger.

"You and Flem have some trouble back yonder?" one
asked in a while.

The stranger ceased chewing. "Back where?" he
said quickly, looking at his interrogator.

"Look like you been nicked," the other explained.
The stranger looked at him quietly, holding his innocent
florid carton. "Yo' year," the man added.

"Oh. That?" The stranger touched his damaged ear
briefly. "That's just a little mistake of mine," he said
easily. "Nothing a tall. I was kind of absent-minded
about picketting them ponies one night. Studyin' about
something and fergot they was one of 'em behind me."
He put another gingersnap into his mouth while the
spectators looked at his ear quietly. "Happen to any
man that aint careful," he added. "But put a little axel
dope on her and you dont notice it. They're pretty
lively, now, lazing along all day doing nothing. It'll

24

work out of 'em in a day or so, though."

"Hmph," grunted a spectator, "Work 'em through a feed chopper if they was mine. That's what I'd do."

"No, no, brother," the stranger protested quickly, "Them's good gentle ponies. Look a here." He approached the herd and extended his hand. The nearest horse dozed on three legs in a kind of watchful dejection. It had mild mismatched eyes and a head shaped like an ironing board, and seemingly without coming awake its long head cropped yellow teeth in a flashing arc and for a moment man and horse seemed hopelessly and inextricably tangled together. "You would, would you, you hammer-headed bastard?" the man said in a repressed earnest tone, then his feet touched the ground again and he half turned with one hand gripping the beast's nostrils and the pony's muzzle completely reversed and pointing skyward. The pony stood and trembled, emitting hoarse smothered sounds.

"See," the owner panted, digging his heels into the soil while the cords of his neck thrust taut under his sunburned skin, "gentle as a dog. All you want to do is handle 'em a little and work 'em like hell for a couple of days, and they'll be gentle as a dog."

"Will you throw yerself in with the hosses, Mister?" a voice asked mildly from the rear of the throng. The man gathered himself and released the pony's muzzle, and as he sprang free a second horse slashed his vest down the back from neck to hem as neatly as ever D'Artagnan could have done it with his rapier, and at this moment Flem Snopes and Jody Varner reappeared.

"Let's git 'em in the lot, Buck," Flem said. He got in the wagon and gathered up the reins, and the

25

stranger with his divided vest flapping from either shoulder put his confection back into his pocket beside the pistol and moved to the rear of the herd while it rolled its wild mismatched eyes at him, and cursed it in a fluent mixture of bastard Spanish and purest Anglo Saxon, and the spectators followed at a respectful distance up the road to Mrs Littlejohn's boarding house and hotel and to the livery barn lot next to it. Someone opened the gate and the wagon passed through, but when the herd of ponies at last comprehended that it was to pass within the wire enclosure its morale disintegrated again and it stood on its collective hind legs and waved its wire-hobbled forelegs with passion. The onlookers fled again and took refuge on the veranda of Mrs Littlejohn's boarding house, and the stranger cursed his herd steadily and then it stood on its forelegs for a while, and the stranger rose to sublime heights, like an apotheosis.

At last he drove them through the gate, and the herd crowded against the wagon and roved its wild assorted eyes and trembled violently. The stranger closed the gate and Flem Snopes descended from the wagon and retired with a fair assumption of deliberation to Mrs Littlejohn's veranda, and the stranger approached the herd. He got into the wagon and with soft cajoleries he drew steadily on the barbed wire hackamore so as to bring the first one up to be released. The horse plunged madly, and sank back against the wire as though it would hang itself out of hand. The contagion passed through the herd and it once more fell to standing on its various ends and waving its unoccupied feet and the horse that was committing suicide sprawled

with its legs at rigid angles and its belly flat on the earth
in an ecstasy of negation. The man desisted.

"Bring me a pair of wire cutters," he shouted to the
group on Mrs Littlejohn's veranda, and one called Eck
detached himself and disappeared into the house and
presently reappeared and crossed the lot warily to the
wagon. "Here," the stranger directed, "jump up here
and keep the slack out of the wire and I'll cut 'em
aloose."

Eck climbed into the wagon and took hold of the
wire hackamore gingerly. "Pull him up, pull him up,"
the stranger said sharply. He grasped the wire himself
and took a turn about one of the wagon stakes with it,
and again the first pony lay passionately back against
it until his tongue protruded and his mad mismatched
eyes started from his head. "Now, hold 'em like that,"
the stranger said, and grasped the wire cutters and lept
into the herd. His Stetson and his flapping severed vest
disappeared in a kaleidoscopic maelstrom of yellow
teeth and rolling eyes and sickling legs from which
there burst one by one like partridges and each wearing
a barbed wire necklace, his mad gaudy charges.

The first one to be freed shot like an arrow across
the lot. It struck the wire fence without any diminution
of speed whatever. The fence gave a little to the shock,
recovered viciously and slammed the horse to earth,
where it lay for a second in a static and wild-eyed frenzy,
then scrambled to its feet and rushed onward in a new
direction, slammed again into the fence and was cast to
earth once more. Meanwhile all were now freed and
they whipped and whirled dizzily about the narrow
enclosure, and from the ultimate dust the stranger

27

emerged and ran for his life. His vest was completely gone now, as was most of his shirt and he weaved through the dizzy calico rushes of the insane beasts, feinting and dodging with the consummate skill of a Red Grange. Eck was still in the wagon bed.

The stranger mounted Mrs Littlejohn's veranda and joined the spectators. The ponies yet streaked like wild fish back and forth through the growing dusk in the lot, but not quite so violently. The stranger detached a fragment of his shirt from beneath his galluses and wiped his face with it and threw it away, and produced his carton and tilted a gingersnap into his hand. "Pretty lively, aint they?" he said, breathing heavily. "But it'll work out of 'em in a couple days. Then you'll have as good a saddle and work pony as you'll want."

There was a polite noncommittal silence. The ponies slid and whipped back and forth along the fence, milling slowly and gradually bunching together. "What'll you pay a feller to take one of 'em off your hands?" a voice asked from the dusk, and a small boy with a round yellow head burrowed among their legs saying, "Popper, popper, where's popper?"

"Who you lookin' fer, sonny?" one asked, and another said: "Hit's Eck Snopes' boy. Eck aint got outen the wagon yit, is he? Oh, Eck!"

Eck in the wagon thrust his head cautiously forth. "Maw's a-waitin' fer us to hitch up an' take out," his son called to him.

That night, beneath the halfmoon, the ponies huddled in the corner of the lot or singly or in pairs rushed in fluid phantom shapes along the fence, returned and huddled again. The idlers lingered later than usual that night on Mrs Littlejohn's veranda overlooking the lot and its splotched huddle from which rose at intervals high abrupt squeals and vicious thudding blows. Flem Snopes had disappeared just before supper time, at home doubtless with his wife and baby, and the stranger was also absent. In a new shirt and a corduroy coat and his pistol and a fresh carton of gingersnaps he was engaged in a poker game in the rear of the livery stable, where he won eleven dollars.

So the loiterers sat in the moonlight and discussed the horses and the stranger and Flem Snopes in their slow grave idiom, speculating on the relations between the three. Meanwhile the moon rose higher, and across the way in an apple tree like a resurgent phantom of old forgotten springs and gustily delicate upon the air, a mockingbird sang.

"First one I've hearn this year," a voice said quietly from the shadowed veranda, and a sewing machine agent rose from his chair and yawned elaborately.

"Well," he said, "You folks can buy them plugs if you want to, but me, I'd jest as soon buy a tiger or a rattlesnake. Jest as soon."

The others sat courteously noncommittal, and the sewing machine agent went on into the house, and presently another man followed him, and then with muttered words the others rose and dispersed slowly through the gathering moon. The houses were all dark at this hour, and soon the last straggler had betaken his shadow away through the silver dust, and there was no sound anywhere in the land save an occasional abrupt

29

squeal or thudding blow from the livery stable lot.

The next morning Buck, the Texan, came to the boarding house door and yawned at the red and hill-nicked rim of the sun. About him the world waked ineffably fresh beneath the spring dawn, waked happily chill, as though not yet fully reassured; and the mockingbird returned to the apple tree across the way and sang again, and the sun heaved up like a captive balloon from beyond the ultimate horizon.

Buck yawned again like a huge luxurious cat and crossed the veranda and approached the lot fence where already stood in patient relaxation three overalled adult figures and a small boy with a round yellow head, quietly watching the ponies as they scraped and snuffed at the dung and dust impregnated chaff of the barn yard.

"Morning, boys," said Buck cheerily, and the three adults turned slowly and responded with grave awkward courtesy, and the boy watched him quietly with two unwinking eyes blue as periwinkles. "Come to git a early pick, have you?" he continued heartily. "Well, they aint a one that aint worth fifteen dollars of any man's money. See that there wall-eyed one with one white year and a rope burn on his off shoulder? And that fiddle headed one with most of his mane gone? Look at them shoulders and legs and pasterns. You know what I'd do in yo' place? I'd snap them two ponies up at twenty-five dollars fer the pair before somebody else comes along and runs the price up at arction, that's what I'd do." He roved his bold inviting eye from one grave face to another, and one by one the faces' owners turned them upon the ponies again.

"We jest come to see 'em," one explained at last. "We aint minded to buy right now."

"Better not put it off too long," Buck said . "Hey, Bud?" The boy had moved quietly behind him and now gazed at the butt of the pistol that protruded from his pocket with rapt silent absorption. "Well, you boys are in time to see 'em eat breakfast, anyways," Buck said. The three men watched him and he followed the fence to the gate and opened it and passed through and closed it again. The ponies immediately ceased snuffing at the ground and stared at him in premonitory alarm with their assorted eyes. Buck drew slowly nearer, and the herd began to disintegrate gaudily.

"Yere, boys," Buck called to the watchers, "Git over in here and help me drive 'em into the barn yonder." The three adults spoke among themselves in low voices, then they moved slowly to the gate. The boy followed, and at the gate his father remarked him. "You stay outside, Ad. One of them things'll bite your head off like it was a acorn." Then the three men entered the lot with palpable reluctance.

"Come on," Buck said impatiently, "They wont stampede no more. They jest aint used to barns and may be a little skittish about goin' in."

"I jest as lief see 'em stay out here, far's I'm concerned," Eck rejoined.

"Well, we'll jest drive 'em inside and give 'em a good bait of feed, and they'll settle down gentle as a milk cow. Git you a stick of some sort—there's a bunch of wagon stakes against the fence there—and if one of 'em tries to rush you, bust him right over the head with it: they're used to being handled that way and they'll

31

know what you mean."

The men armed themselves with the wagon stakes, and the ponies huddled restively and rolled their eyes, and Eck's son, Admiral Dewey, came unobserved into the lot. Smoke now rose from Mrs Littlejohn's kitchen, and breakfastsounds came forth upon the immaculate morning air, and Mrs Littlejohn herself in an apron and an armful of stovewood stood in the kitchen yard and watched them, and other overalled men appeared from nowhere and leaned quietly against the fence.

Buck distributed his helpers fanwise and they advanced upon the huddle which broke gradually into fluid gaudy individuals turning upon themselves ceaselessly though not yet running. Buck cursed them in a steady cheerful voice. "Dont hurry 'em, now. Git in there, you banjo-faced jack rabbit. Let 'em take their time, and they'll go in all right. Whooey, now. Git in there."

Admiral Dewey brought his innocent yellow thatch and his azure eyes yet closer, raptly and profoundly entranced and yet unobserved. The ponies trembled and huddled and fell slowly back, still watching the men. At intervals one feinted to break away, but Buck immediately and skillfully hit him with a piece of dirt or a rock, whereupon he burrowed toward the center and thrust another horse into his former place. Then one in the rear of the huddle saw the barn door just behind him and whirled and snorted, and the others whirled also, but before they could break Buck tore the wagon stake from Eck's hand and accompanied by the more valorous of Eck's two friends, rushed forward and laid about him on heads and shoulders, so that when the break did

come, it swept the herd into the barn in a rushing
thunder of hooves that brought up against the rear
wall with a crash.

"Seems to've held, all right." Buck and the other
man slammed the half length doors to and they gazed
over the door into the tunnel of the barn at the far
end of which the ponies were a shapeless huddle of
splotched phantom shapes in the obscurity. "Yep, it
held, all right." Eck and the third man came up and
gazed over the door, and the boy followed quietly and
glued his round yellow head to a crack and his father
remarked him again.

"Aint I tole you to keep outen here?" Eck demanded. "Them critters'll kill you quicker'n you can say scat.
You go on and git outside that fence, now."

"Lemme stay, paw," the boy said. "I want to see
them circus hosses too."

"Well," Eck relented. "But you stay clost to me, now,
you hear?"

"Whyn't you git yo' paw to buy you one of 'em, Ad?"
the second man suggested.

"Me buy one of them critters," Eck rejoined, "when
I kin go to the creek anytime and ketch a snappin'
turtle or a moccasin fer nothin'?"

Buck had opened the doors and slipped into the
barn and the first man had shut the doors behind him
and dropped the bar into the slots, and they could now
hear Buck busy in the corn crib. The ponies huddled
like gaudy ghosts in the remote gloom, passive and
watchful. Then one by one they grew quieter and
lowered their heads and nuzzled and sniffed into a long
feeding trough worn silken smooth by generations of

prehensile lips, that was attached to the rear wall. Buck reappeared in the door to the feed room. "I cant find nothing but shell corn," he said. "Aint they got no year corn, you reckon?"

"I reckon not," Eck said after a while. "Boatner dont usually use no year corn. Wont they eat shell corn?"

"I reckon they'll eat it all right, when they get used to it," Buck answered. "They aint never seen no shelled corn before." He retired into the feed room and presently sounds of labor came therefrom, and a dry rattling of grain into metal receptacles, and he reappeared once more with a metal bucket full of shelled corn in either hand and retreated into the gloom toward the parti-colored rumps of his charges. The three men stood quietly gazing over the door.

Buck vanished into the gloom and a subdued intimation of alarm, uttering soothing and profane words. Then again a dry rattling of hard pellets on a wood surface, a sound broken by a snort of purest emotion, and the obscurity of the barn became abruptly thunderous and a plank cracked with a sharp report, and as the three peered across the door the dark interior evolved into mad tossing shapes like gaudy flames downrushing.

"Come on yere, Ad," Eck roared, and his two companions turned with him and fled to the refuge of the wagon bed. The barn door disintegrated into matchwood before the tide, and the beasts rushed forth like a towering parti-colored wave full of glaring eyes and wild yellow teeth, rushed forth and whelmed and utterly obscured Admiral Dewey where he yet stood in the middle of the doorway, rushed on and became single atoms whirling and dashing about the lot, reveal-

35

ing at last Admiral Dewey's yellow astonished head
and his diminutive faded overalls still motionless and
untouched in the center of the doorway.

"You, Ad!" his father roared again, and Admiral
Dewey turned and ran toward the wagon, and two of
the frenzied beasts rushed up quartering and galloped
all over him without touching him and he came on and
his father leaned down and snatched him into the wagon
by one arm and slammed him bottom upward across
his knees and fumbled for a coiled hitching rope in the
bottom of the wagon bed with a hand that trembled.
"Aint I told you not to come in here? Aint I told you?"
Eck's suntanned skin was a sickly white and his voice
shook with fear and relief and rage and he picked up
the hitchrein and doubled it.

"Ow, paw; ow, paw," Admiral Dewey protested,
writhing his hands palm outward across his young
behind, "Ow, paw!"

"Aint I told you?" Eck repeated whitely, laying on
Admiral Dewey with the doubled rope, "Aint I told
you?" Admiral Dewey lifted his voice and wept, and
his father presently exhausted his justified paternal
relief and the boy wriggled free and tenderly caressed
his diminutive overalls with two dirty hands, and
presently his tribulation had passed away and beneath
his pale golden thatch his periwinkle eyes were like
two patches of spring sky after rain. Buck stood in the
shattered door and shook a gingersnap into his hand
and tossed the carton away. The mad rushing of the
ponies had diminished and they now trotted about on
high stiff legs, tossing their rolling various eyes. "I
doubted that there shelled corn right along," he said

36

generally and Mrs Littlejohn came onto her veranda and rang a heavy hand bell.

"Chuck wagon," Buck said. "You boys stick around: arction begins right after breakfast." He strode across the lot and the horses watched him and slid from his path in gaudy fluid flashes, and those in the wagon descended hurriedly and Eck caught up his son and they followed Buck briskly across the lot. The fence was fairly well lined with quiet overalled figures in patient restful attitudes and along the road wagons stood, with their teams reversed and tied to the wagon wheels and saddled horses nibbled at the trunk of the apple tree. "Arction begins right after breakfast," Buck repeated to them and he closed the gate and went on into Mrs Littlejohn's house. As he passed from sight another wagon drove up and a man descended and joined the spectators where they stood or squatted along the fence, talking quietly among themselves.

"Yere, Buddy—" Buck sitting on top of the gate post dug terrifically into his corduroy pants and then creased his flourishing belly toward Admiral Dewey's innocent straw-thatched admiration "—run over to the sto' and git me a box of gingersnaps. Now, boys, who'll start her off with a bid? Come on, now, step right up: they's plenty fer ever'body, but the fust ones gits the best pick. Take your choice and make yo' bid, boys. They aint a hoss in that lot that aint worth fifteen dollars. Young, sound in wind and limb, good fer saddle or work stock; outlast fo' ordinary hosses: you cant kill one of 'em with a axel tree. Look at that one with three sock feet and the frost bit years; watch 'im now when they passes here again. Look at that there shoulder action. That hoss is worth twenty dollars if he's worth a cent. Now, who'll make me a bid on him to start the ball a-rollin'? Come on, boys, who'll—" (an unidentified voice: "Fo' bits") "—make me a bid on 'im? Watch 'im good; look at the way he totes his head: lively as any stable-raised hoss anywher'. Or if he dont suit, how about that there fiddle-headed one without no mane— how about him? Fer a feller that wants a good saddle pony, I'd ruther have him than the other'n. Come on now: I heard somebody say fifty cents jest then. Hey, brother, you meant five dollars, didn't you? Do I year five—Much obliged, buddy." He bent and received his paper tube from Admiral Dewey. "—five dollars? Speak up, brother. Do I year five dollars?" Buck cupped his ear toward the grave noncommittal spectators standing along the fence. The ponies clotted at the far side of the lot, watching the people with flying vari-colored eyes, broke into stiffly trotting nervous shapes,

38

huddled again.

"Fo' bits fer the lot," the unidentified voice repeated. Buck laughed with theatrical gusto.

"Har, har, that's a good 'un," he said. "Fifty cents fer the dried mud off of 'em, he means. Who'll give a dollar mo' fer the genu-wine Texas cuckleburrs? Har, har, that's a good 'un." Then his voice became pleading, confidential: "Look a yere, boys, is that any way to talk about them hosses? Look at 'em, and tell me if this country ever seen a better collection of livestock at dirt cheap prices. Hey, Grampaw,"— he bent and shouted hoarsely at a bearded ancient with a gutta-percha ear-trumpet coiled like an inert serpent about his neck—"tell 'em if you ever seen a better looking bunch of stock at public arction in this town?" A bystander attracted the ancient's attention, and he uncoiled his black tube with deliberation and inserted one end into his ear. But Buck's attention had flown on and he embraced them all with his hoarse exhortation. "Come on, boys: start her off, now. Who'll pick a hoss and make a bid? Yere, Eck, you been helpin' me and you know them hosses. How about makin' a bid on that there wall-eyed one with the rope-burn you picked out this mawnin'? Look at that hawss, boys: watch 'im now when he comes by again. Yere, wait a minute." Buck slid easily into the pen. The ponics broke before his approach and slid stiffly away along the fence, but Buck with his quenchless faith in his invulnerability rushed without haste among them and efficiently cut out the wall-eyed one and drove it into the fence corner, and when it whirled and rushed at him with a kind of wild and fatal desperation, he struck it between the eyes

39

with the butt of his pistol and felled it and lept immediately upon its prone and lolling head.

The pony recovered almost at once and pawed its
gaudy body to its knees and heaved at its prisoned head
and fought itself erect and dragged Buck up also and
waved him violently like a rag. The commotion envel-
oped itself in dust and it moved terrifically along the
fence through which the overalled spectators watched
with a passive and sober interest, then Buck brought
the beast to a standstill and held it with one hand clamp-
ing its nostrils and its muzzle twisted backward across
its scarred neck, while labored groans rumbled hollowly
within it.

"Look him over, boys," Buck panted, turning his
suffused face and the popping glare of his eyes toward
the spectators, "Look him over, quick. Them shoulders
and hocks—" the pony's trembling rigidity exploded
again "—and laigs you bastard I'll tear yo' face right
look 'im over quick boys yere yere goddam wuth fifteen
dollars of lemme git a holt of my whoa Whoa who'll
make me a bid for God's Whoa you blare-eyed jack
rabbit!" Buck's voice rose in an unbroken stream from
the center of a calico maelstrom upon whose ceaseless
orbit his suspender metals gleamed in fleeting glints.
Then his clay-colored Stetson soared deliberately, and
immediately afterward, Buck himself, though not so
deliberately, and the pony shot free in mad stag-like
bounds. Buck picked up his hat and returned, dusting
himself off, and mounted his post again, breathing
heavily.

"Now, boys," he said, and a wagon with a man and a
woman in it stopped in the road and the man descended

40

and joined the throng. "Come up, brother, you're in plenty of time," Buck greeted him heartily. "Now, boys, who says that hoss aint worth fifteen dollars? Why you couldn't buy that much dynamite fer fifteen dollars. Look a yere, boys, they aint a one of 'em cant do a mile in fo' minutes; work 'em like hell all day, then turn 'em into the pasture and they'll boa'd themselves; whenever you think about it, lay 'em over the head with a single tree, and after a couple of days every bastard one'll be so gentle you'll have to put 'em outen the house at night like a cat." He refreshed himself with a gingersnap and raised his voice again, and the woman sitting in the wagon descended gauntly in faded calico and a man's broken shoes and came among them and touched her husband's arm.

"Henery," she said in a flat voice.

The man turned his head over his shoulder. "Git back to that waggin," he said.

"Yere, Missis," Buck said, "Henry's a-goin' to git the bargain of his life, in a minute now. Yere, boys, let missis git up to the fence wher' she kin see. Come on, now, Henry, yere's yo' chance to pick out missis that saddle hoss she's been a-wantin'. Who says fifteen—"

"Henery," the woman said again without raising her voice, and she laid her gnarled hand on her husband's sleeve.

"Git on, now, like I tole you," the man repeated harshly, shaking off her hand.

"He haint no more despair'n to buy one of them things," the woman said generally and without heat, in a voice at once patient and hopeless and grave, "and we'uns not five dollars ahead of the po' house, he haint

41

no more despair."

"Shut yo' mouth, and git on back to that waggin,'" the man said with cold fury. "Do you want I taken a stick to you right yere in the road?"

The bystanders stood and lounged, quietly incurious. Buck cleared his throat loudly. "How about that hoss, Eck? Make me a bid and git 'em to goin'. Ten dollars? How about a ten dollar bid, Eck?"

"What use I got fer a hoss I'd need a bear-trap to ketch?" Eck rejoined.

"Ketch them hosses?" Buck repeated with hearty astonishment, "Why, Bud hisself yere can ketch any of them hosses with a little practice. Didn't you jest see me ketch one of 'em?"

"Yeah," Eck agreed drily, "I seen you. And I dont want nothin' as big as a hoss if I got to wrastle with it ever' time me and it's on the same side of the fence."

"Har, har," Buck roared without mirth, "listen to Eck, boys. He wants a piece of crow-bait he'll have to prop up again' the fence ever' time he stops, I reckon. Now, listen yere, Eck: I tell you what I'll do, to git the arction goin': I'll give you that wall-eyed hoss if you'll start the biddin' on the next 'un. How about it? "

Eck considered for a while. The others stood or lounged, quietly attentive. "I jest starts the biddin'," Eck said at last. "I dont have to buy lessen I aint over-topped?"

"Sure, sure, " Buck agreed. "Year that, boys? That there wall-eyed hoss with the scar neck is Eck's hoss: I'm a-givin' it to him. All right, boys: let's go. See that there pony that looks like he's had his haid in a flour bar'l? Yere he goes, there. Wuth fifteen dollars of any

42

man's money. All right, Eck: whatcha goin' to say?
Ten dollars?"

"A dollar," Eck said.

"One dollar?" repeated Buck. "One dollar? I sho'ly
never heard that right, Eck. Why, a dollar wont pay
fer the vest that hoss cut offen me yistiddy. Look a
yere—"

"Dang it," Eck said, "Two dollars, then."

"Y'all are foolin', boys. I ask you, now: Is that any
way fer a man to act at a arction sale of livestock guaran-
teed sound and hearty and willin'? Two dollars is bid:
I got to except it, but are you boys goin' to stand thar
and see Eck git two hosses fer a dollar a head? Air you?"

"Three dollars," the husband said, and his wife tried
to pull him away and he flung her hand off, and she
folded her hands across her lank stomach: a quiet
tragic figure with eyes that saw nothing and held
nothing but the dead ashes of an instinct become
habitual and compulsory. "Misters," she said in her flat
emotionless voice, "Misters, we got chaps in the house,
and not cawn to feed the stock we got, and five dollars
I earnt a-weavin' atter dark and him a-sleepin' in the
bed and he haint no more despair."

"Henry bids three dollars," Buck shouted. "Raise
him a dollar, Eck, and you got two ponies at two dollars
a haid."

Eck considered a while.

"Henery," the woman said again, with her dull and
infinite patience. The man, glaring at Eck, paid her no
heed.

"Fo' dollars," Eck said.

"Five dollars," the husband shouted, holding aloft

43

his closed fist.

"Mister," the woman said without passion, and she raised her gaunt face and looked at Buck soberly with her faded and empty eyes, "Ef you takes that five dollars I earnt my chaps a-weavin', fer one of them hosses, hit'll be a curse onto you and your'n durin' all the time of man."

"Five dollars," the husband shouted again. He shoved himself to the fence and raised his closed hand to the level of Buck's knees and opened it and revealed a wadded mass of worn bills and silver. "And the feller that raises it'll beat my head off, er I'll beat his'n."

"Yere, Bud," said Buck in a hoarse whisper, "run over to the sto' and git me a box of gingersnaps." Again the sun came level across the earth and into the apple tree among the blooms and bees and upon the wagons lined along the road, and the horses and mules tethered among them and among the locust trees. Buck yet on his gate post, the loungers in faded negligent blue in easy inert attitudes beyond the spaces between whose heads, ceaseless fluid gleams like gaudy and patched calico. Admiral Dewey's diminutive overalls trotted, a little wearily now, up the road to the store; in their battered and weathered wagon, behind two abject and somnolent bone-racks, Henry's wife in her dun shapeless garment and sunbonnet sat quietly, a figure of patient and tragic despair. On a wire stretching from a china-berry tree to Mrs Littlejohn's back porch, assorted garments dangled laxly and heavily damp. Smoke no longer rose from beneath the blackened pot, and the half hogshead lay propped on its edge against the

44

wooden block. Beside it the scrubbing board glinted
its metal ridges.

Buck had sold all but two of his beasts for prices
ranging from a dollar and seventy-five cents to eight
dollars, and he climbed wearily and stiffly from his fence
post and stamped his feet into his boots and removed his
hat and mopped his brow with his sleeve. The beasts
were weary too, after the long foodless day of sunlight
and voices in monotonous rise and fall and quiet con-
stant human faces watching them always. Above, the
bowl of the sky hushed itself into mysterious ineffable
azures, and the apple tree where tethered horses
stamped and gnawed was like a candelabra tinged faintly
with pink and gold. No mockingbird, though. The
bystanders stood and lounged timelessly and patiently
one with the grave rythm of the earth, talking among
themselves in sparse monosyllables. Except Henry, the
husband. His voice alone went on in flat nasal repetition:
a sort of querulous and savage impatience.

"I bought a hoss and I paid cash," he said again, harshly belligerent, shouldering himself among passive faded blue shirts nearer the auctioneer, "And yit you expect me to stand around yere twell they's all sold. Well you kin do all the expectin' you wants: I'm a-goin' to take my hoss outen there and git on home. What about it?"

"Take yo' hoss, then," Buck answered coldly, and their glances clashed, and it was Henry who looked away. He stood with his head slightly bowed, tasting despair and rage, swallowing it like a delicate warm salt, brooding his baffled eyes upon the drooping gaudy huddle of the beasts without seeing them.

"Aint you a-goin' to ketch him fer me?" he asked presently in a quiet tone.

"He aint my hoss," Buck answered softly, watching Henry's working profile steadily, and it was as though he had gone completely away from behind his still unwinking eyes. Admiral Dewey returned at his weary unflagging trot and gave Buck the fresh box and Buck, still watching Henry with grave detachment, ripped the end from the box and shook five or six of the cakes into his hand and gave them to Admiral Dewey. "Much obliged, bud."

A stillness had fallen upon the group, upon its easy unchanged attitudes. Henry stood again with his head bowed a little in an isolation of impotence. Then he raised his head. "Who'll he'p me ketch my hoss?" he asked in a dry light voice. None moved. The sun hung without heat in the western sky, the lower part of the rim flattening with perspective. The level shadow of Mrs Littlejohn's house advanced across the lot and

46

overtook the weary huddle of the ponies, climbed the barn wall and there lost itself. Smoke rose in the still air from the kitchen, and supper sounds; and sparrows swept in a garrulous cloud across the lot to roost in the barn and sat in a row along the eaves for a while before turning in, and in the high mysterious blue swallows twittered and stooped and whirled in erratic indecision.

"Bring that there plow-line over yere." The man raised his voice a little, and the woman descended obediently from the wagon and reached a new coiled cotton rope out of it and came to her husband. The man took the rope from her and shouldered himself toward the gate, without raising his head. Buck was in his path and the man went around him and Buck watched the man with his quiet detached stare. "Come on yere," the man said gruffly, and the woman moved again and followed.

"Dont go in there, missus," Buck said without emphasis, and the woman stopped. The man opened the gate and entered, then he turned with his hand still on the gate, but without raising his eyes. "Come on yere," he repeated.

"Dont you go in there, missis," Buck said again, without any inflection whatever. The woman stood quietly between them: it was as though she had left her body for the time.

"I reckon I better," she said presently, and she followed her husband into the lot and he shut the gate behind them. The spectators stood or lounged quietly, their eyes bent on the ground as though in rapt contemplation. The man advanced toward the ponies, and the woman followed like an automaton, and the spectators watched them quietly across the fence, and the horses

47

huddled and blended and moved intricately among
themselves and shifted on the point of disintegration.
The man shouted curses at them and advanced slowly
and the woman followed step for step, then the huddle
broke and the beasts slid on high stiff legs around them,
and they followed with a dull implacable patience.
"Now," the man said, "Thar he is: get 'im into that
corner." The horse slid its stiff legs and the woman
shouted at it and it spun, but the man hit it over the
head with his coiled rope and it whirled again and
slammed into the angle of the fence. "Keep 'im in there,
now," the man said, and he approached gradually. The
horse watched him with wild glaring eyes, then it
rushed again. The woman shouted at it and waved her
arms, but it soared past her in long bounds; and again
they followed it patiently and hemmed it up again,
and again it rushed past the woman's outflung arms.
Then the man turned and struck the woman with
the coiled rope. "Why didn't you head it?" he said,
"Why didn't you?" and he struck her again. Those
along the fence stood quietly, brooding on the earth
at their feet.

Buck entered the lot and Flem Snopes appeared
among the bystanders chewing steadily. One or two
greeted him and he responded and spat and gazed
quietly into the lot. Buck strode quickly to the man and
caught the rope from his upraised hand. The man
whirled and made to spring, but the spring never came
and he crouched with his dangling arms by his side and
his half-mad gaze on Buck's feet. The woman stood
quietly, and it was as though she were in another place.
Then Buck took the man's trembling arm and led him

to the gate, and the woman followed, and Buck opened
the gate and thrust the man through it and held it open
until the woman had passed through.

"Here, missis," Buck said. He dragged a mass of
bills from his pocket and took a five dollar bill from it
and put it into her slow hand. "Git him into yo' waggin
and git him on home."

"What's that fer, Buck?" Flem asked.

"Thinks he bought one of them ponies," Buck
answered. "Take him on, missis."

"Give 'im that there money back," the husband said.
He was trembling. Below the frayed cuffs of his homemade calico shirt his hands shut and opened against his
flanks. "Give it back to him."

"Git him on away, missis," Buck repeated.

"You take yo' money and I take my hoss," the man
said. "I bought that hoss and I aim to have him if I got
to shoot him."

"You dont own no hoss of mine," Buck said tone-
lessly. "Git him away, missis."

The man raised his wild face. His shaking hand
reached for the bill. The woman did not move her hand
while he fumbled at it, and at last he drew the bill from
her hand. "It's my hoss," the man said. "I bought it.
These fellers seen me. I paid fer it. It's my hoss. Yere,"
he said, and he offered the bill to Flem Snopes. "You
got somethin' to do with these hosses. I bought one.
Here's the money, see? I bought one. Ask him."

Flem took the bill and put it in his pocket. The
spectators stood gravely attentive in relaxed attitudes.
The woman crossed her hands patiently on her lank
stomach while evening came yet more, accomplishing

49

itself.

"Flem'll have it fer you tomorrow," Buck said gently. "He dont own none of them hosses. Better git back to yo' waggin." The woman turned obediently and returned to the wagon and mounted and sat quietly in the dusk. But her husband merged again into the throng.

"How many you got left?" Flem asked.

"Got two. Swap 'em both and the waggin fer a buckboa'd. Who'll make a good trade quick?"

They considered gravely. Presently one spoke.

"I got a buggy I'll swap you that-a-way. 'Taint right new."

"Got fo' wheels?" Buck asked.

"Sure," the man replied. "Thar 'tis acrosst the road."

It wasn't new, but it had four wheels, and the man went over and untethered his mules from the wheels of it and dragged it across the road. "It'll do," Buck said briefly, and he entered the lot again and the ponies slid away from him and circled and clotted and he entered the barn and reappeared presently with his coat over his arm and leading his driving horses. He paused at the wagon and reached his blanket roll out and came on and the ponies fled before him again circling and huddled and watched him with their various eyes. The bystanders helped him hitch his team to the buggy, then he mounted to the seat.

"Well, so long, boys," he said. "Glad to've saw you."

"Wher' you headin' fer now? Back to Texas?" Eck asked.

"I guess not," Buck answered. "Not right away. I reckon I'll go and have a look-see at them nawthun

50

towns while I'm yere. Washington and Noo Yawk and Philadelphy. Time enough fer Texas after that. Well, remember about bustin' them ponies over the haid occasionally till they gits used to you. Then you wont have no trouble with 'em. Them's bargains, boys. Well—" he gathered up the reins again but he said Whoa immediately. "Yere, bud," he dug into his pocket again, "run over to the sto—Ne'mine: I'll go by thar my self. You better stay and he'p yo' paw git his hosses home."

"I'll ride as fer as the sto' with you," Flem Snopes said, climbing into the seat.

"Git up there." The buggy moved forward and Buck slanted his Stetson forward and jerked his hand in casual farewell. "Take keer of yo'selves."

"Well," said Eck after a while, "whut are we a-waitin' fer? fer'm to go to roost like chickens?"

Evening was completely accomplished. The sparrows had gone, and the final cloud of swallows had swirled into a chimney somewhere and the ultimate celestial edges of the world rolled on into vague and intricate subtleties of softest pearl. The apple tree was a ghost in pearl also, gustily and hauntingly sweet, and the horses tethered beneath it were stamping shapes without bulk or emphasis. In her weathered and fading wagon the woman sat quietly, patient and tragic as a figure out of Sophocles. Mrs Littlejohn came to her door and clanged the heavy handbell and the throng beside the fence stirred slowly while the ponies in the lot, twenty-four hours without food, ceased pawing and snuffing at the matted chaff to watch them.

51

"We better git our ropes," one said at last. "Ever'-body git a rope."

"Wher's our'n, Ad?" Eck prompted. "Go git it."

Admiral Dewey departed obediently and trotted wearily and indefatigably to where their wagon was hitched and got the rope, and others repaired to their various conveyances and returned with various ropes, and still others had no ropes and headed by the clerk, I.O. Snopes, departed in a quiet clump to Jody Varner's store and there purchased rope by kerosene light amid old grave odors of cheese and leather and fecundated earth and returned; and Mrs Littlejohn came to her door and rang the bell again, but none paid her heed. Overhead, in the mysterious ineffable windless with pearl convolvulae, stars. Beyond the west the sun was a fading coal. The ponies huddled like phantom splotched fish in the violet lambence of the lot. Moon presently. Already it was a serene ghost overhead.

They gathered at the gate, with their ropes. From the now shapeless clump of beasts against the barn there came stamping sounds and expulsions of breath. "I reckon," one suggested, "we better all take and ketch 'em one to a time, hadn't we?"

"One to a time," said Henry savagely, and he cursed with slow impotent rage, "After I've stood around yere all day, waiting fer that—" he cursed again, in a kind of spent fever of despair, and his hands knotted in the moonlight upon the fastening of the gate and tugged at it and shook it and tugged at it. From Mrs Littlejohn's came a subdued clashing of cutlery, and an anonymous one filled the yellow door to the kitchen and stood there.

At last Henry opened the gate, and passed through

52

it and the others followed. A beast snorted from their shapeless huddle, and the huddled shifted without breaking. Eck took the rope from his son, and Admiral Dewey pressed on behind his father.

"Yere," Eck said, "You wait out yere."

"Aw, paw," Admiral Dewey protested.

"You wait out yere," Eck repeated firmly. "You been run over twicet today, already."

"Aw, paw. Lemme he'p to ketch our'n. We got two to ketch," he added diabolically.

"That's right," Eck said, "We air got two, aint we?"

"Lemme he'p, paw," Admiral Dewey pressed his advantage.

"Well," his father agreed dubiously. "But you stay clost to me, you year? Ef you gits in front of them varmints again like you done this morning, I dont know whut I'll do to you, but I'll sho' do it."

The others with their ropes formed themselves into a tentative and reluctant fan, without enthusiasm. The ponies stood utterly motionless but restive, watching them, gaudy in the waxing moon. That one emptied Mrs Littlejohn's yellow kitchen door and emerged into the silver wanness and removed the nearest washed garment from the invisible line, stopped in midgesture and looked into the lot again. Eck and his son came up and a man glanced quickly at them.

"Git that 'ere boy outen yere," he commanded.

"Git in the wagon, Ad," Eck directed, and Admiral Dewey obediently trotted on and climbed into the wagon bed.

"Watch 'em clost, now boys," some one advised. "Ef we kin jest git 'em into the barn—" But at that mo-

53

ment the herd broke without haste and parted, and flowed along the rear fence, gathering impetus. "Whooey," one called, and he was answered from the other end of the fan, and another said: "Ther's mine: ther' he is!" and a third, earnestly: "Whooey, head 'em back, there!" They headed the beasts and turned them back, and they merged and slid and spun in short rushes, whirled again back upon themselves. "Whooey! Hold 'em, now! Dont let 'em git by, and we got 'em."

That one in Mrs Littlejohn's yard gathered another garment and stood again, blanched in the gathering moon, swept down a third garment and paused again, and Eck looked behind him swiftly and remarked his son. "Aint I tole you to git in that waggin and stay ther'?" he demanded.

"Look out, paw!" Admiral Dewey exclaimed, "Ther' he is! See 'im?" It was the one Buck had given him: with mutual and unspoken design they had both delegated to temporary abeyance the one Eck had paid money for. "Ketch 'im, paw!"

"Git outen my way, Ad," Eck said. "Whooey." The beasts milled and clotted. The fan contracted cautiously, forcing the beasts toward the splintered and gaping door of the barn. "Whooey. Watch 'em, fellers!" The animals gave back step by step. Occasionally one feinted to rush away but was shouted back, and slowly and gradually the seething huddle fell back into the barn. "Now we got 'em!" one said with repressed exultation, "Whooey! Git in ther'!"

Then the shadow of the barn door fell upon the clotting of animals and an indescribable sound of desperation rose from among them and the men whirled

54

and lept madly before the wild vomit of the yawning barn. But the tide overtook them before they could scatter and hurled two men to earth and rushed on and those aligned outside the fence turned and ran in both directions down the road and a voice rose hoarsely from the lot. "Who in hell lef' that 'ere gate open?"

But open it was, and the mad animals rushed through it and thundered among the somnolent patient beasts tethered to the motionless wagons across the road, and these too became imbued with the mad contagion and sprang and lunged and snapped their hitch-reins amid squeals and thudding blows, and the mass whirled and crashed indescribably among the wagons and eddied about that one where sat Henry's wife like a timeless and symbolic figure out of Greek tragedy and rushed on and overtook the fleeing spectators who turned and threw things at it in wild and hopeless desperation and turned it temporarily.

Eck picked himself from the dust and with Admiral Dewey behind him he ran to the gate and into the road and saw the horse Buck had given him whirl and dash back and whirl and rush up onto Mrs Littlejohn's veranda. "Ther' he goes, paw!" Admiral Dewey shouted thinly, "Into the house ther'!" and they galloped up onto the veranda in time to see the horse rush into a room containing a kerosene lamp and a sewing machine agent in his underclothes, neither of which the pony had probably ever seen before. The sewing machine agent was called V.K. Suratt and he now leaned from the window with one sock on and the other in his hand. He looked swiftly over his shoulder and he and the horse glared at each other for a wild instant, then he sprang out of the window and the pony whirled from the room and rushed on through the hall and onto the back porch just as Mrs Littlejohn, carrying an armful of yet damp clothing and a scrubbing board, mounted onto it.

"Git out of here, you son of a bitch," Mrs Littlejohn said immediately, and her scrubbing board divided neatly on the beast's long evil face, and it whirled and rushed back into the hall, and upon Eck and Admiral Dewey.

"Git to hell outen yere, Ad!" Eck roared in unwitting paraphrase and fell flat, and the pony soared over his prone body and over Admiral Dewey's innocent yellow head and the round and azure astonishment of his eyes, and rushed on to the veranda, where it met V.K. Suratt in his underclothes and still carrying his sock, mounting the steps. It whirled without breaking its stride and rushed to the end of the veranda and soared like a bird outward and into the lot again and on through the open gate and among the disrupted wagons and down the road. The road gashed quietly across the spring-quick land, and crashings and brief thunders and cries and rumors of earnest alarm came across the land, retreating swiftly, and the beast galloped madly on trampling its shadow beneath the yet unleafed trees, rushed on down the road where it curved descending between fledged greening willows brooding tenderly in the moon, to the bridge over the creek.

The bridge was of wood, just wide enough for a single vehicle, and it was occupied at the moment by a farmer's wagon drawn by two somnolent and rythmic mules and containing the farmer's family and an odd

56

cousin or so in split-bottom chairs, returning peace-
fully and drowsily through the moonlight from market-
day in Jefferson. None of these awaked until the pony
was upon them, nor did the beast check or swerve. It
thundered once on the wooden planking of the bridge
and rushed between the slumbering mules, and these
waked madly in opposite directions, and the pony
scrambled onto the wagon tongue and the mules
whirled in unison and the farmer shouted hoarsely and
struck at the pony with his whip and the bridge rail
cracked forlornly amid tilting chairs and the pony scrambled on across the frenzied back of one of the mules and
the farmer rose and kicked at its glaring long face. Then
the wagon lurched downward and hurled the farmer
backward among the stiff inverted finery of his wife
and daughters and cousins and the pony plunged on
and thundered on the plank flooring of the bridge again
and the wagon lurched again and rose, its direction
reversed, and the farmer clawed up the reins again,
shouting, just as the mules finally kicked themselves
free of the wagon and jerked him bodily out of it. He
struck the bridge on his face and was dragged for a few
yards before he could release the reins. Far up the road,
swiftly distancing the high-eared frantic mules, the
pony faded swiftly: a gaudy rushing phantom beneath
the moon.

While they were removing dirt and blood and bridge
fragments from the farmer, one in overalls came up trotting and carrying a rope, and followed by a diminutive
and weary but indefatigable replica of itself.

"Wher'd he go?" asked Eck, panting a little.

They gathered Henry gently out of the trampled
chaff and carried him carefully across the lot and into
Mrs Littlejohn's back yard and across it beneath the
moon drenched china-berry trees. Henry's face was
blanched and stony where death had brushed him with
a casual feather, his eyes were closed and the lax weight
of his head drew his throat in a long profundity from
the torn collar of his shirt, and his teeth glinted dully
beneath the lifted pallor of his lip. But he was not dead
and they stumbled on with repressed breathing, kicking
their own ankles awkwardly, and one trotted with short
plunging steps to support his head, and Mrs Littlejohn's
house was sonorous with a fading thunder and then
from the end of the veranda something soared into the
moon like an unbelievable and wingless goblin in a
nightmare.

"Ther's one mo' of 'em," the head-supporter panted,
and they stumbled on with Henry across the blanched
barren dooryard and onto the shadow of the back porch.

Mrs Littlejohn paused and turned, with her
broken scrubbing board in her hand and her armful
of clothes. She laid the scrubbing board down and
raised the hall lamp from its place on top of the yellow
varnished melodeon. "Bring him in here," she
commanded, thrusting a door open with her knee and
preceding them and they followed her with clumsy
scufflings and laid Henry carefully and awkwardly on
the bed, and Mrs Littlejohn set the lamp down and
looked briefly at Henry's bloodless face. "I'll declare,
you men," she said and they stood quietly and she said:
"Better tell his wife," and went out, and they looked at
Henry and shuffled their feet and muttered among

themselves. You go. No, you better go. Let Ernest git her. Go tell her, Ernest.

Ernest departed and they shifted clumsily, watching Henry's calm face, and their monstrous shadows aped them on the wall and Mrs Littlejohn returned without her armful of clothes and with a blackened kettle and some cloths, and then Henry's wife came into the room with her desolate dog's eyes and stood at the foot of the bed with her worn hands clasped across her shapeless lank garment and her face in shadow.

"Git outen the way," Mrs Littlejohn said without heat, and they moved with clumsy footsounds and agitated their shapeless shadows on the wall, and Mrs Littlejohn set the kettle on a chair and shook out one of the cloths. "Git on outside," she repeated. "See ef you cant find nothing to play with that wont kill none of ye." The men moved obediently on awkward tiptoe. "Tell Will Varner to come over here," she added. "I reckon a man aint so different from a mule, come long or short."

They tiptoed through the dark hallway and onto the veranda, into the pallid refulgence of the moon. The apple tree raised its virginal transience, haunting as a forgotten strain of music frozen into fragile and fleeting permanence, still as a dream, as austere and passionate and fine. From the immeasurable distance and sourceless, voices in indistinguishable sounds; the brief rushing thunder of hooves on a remote wooden bridge and a cry grave and earnest and clear as a far bell in falling suspense: "Whooey! Head 'im!"

"Ther's another of 'em," one said, and they stood in their easy identical overalls, listening, hearing across

60

the mysterious mooned land other cries and nameless
sounds, sourceless and originless as bubbles in water.
Then Henry screamed from the mellow subdued lumi-
nosity down the dark hall behind them and they remained
motionless and with bent heads, and the scream sank
to a harsh respiratory Ah. Ah. Ah. on a rising note that
again became emasculate. We better git Varner they
said among themselves. We better git Uncle Billy.

They descended the steps quietly and together and
went in a body through the blanched dust to Uncle
Billy Varner's house and Henry quit screaming and they
reached Uncle Billy's and stood in the moonlight in his
front yard and called him. Presently he replied from a
window and they explained their errand and Uncle
Billy leaned outward on his braced nightshirted arm,
gazing out across the moon-mad world wild and hushed
and sad with spring.

"Whooey. Head 'im, ther'." Strophe and antistrophe;
clear and remote; dramatic and sourcleess and without
meaning.

"Air they still a-tryin' to ketch them dang rabbits?"
Uncle Billy said, and he drew his head in and descended
presently, buttoning his pants over his nightshirt and
slipping on his coat from beneath which his braces dangled in twin loops.

"Yes, sir, they're still a-tryin'," he said again, and
they tramped their skulking shadows in the silver dust
and leafless trees but no longer immaculate soared
upward finely thinned and delicate. "Whooey."

"Well, hit's a good night fer it," he said again.
"Bright as day. My, my, that 'ere apple ought to bear
this year, sho'."

61

"Make cawn grow, too, ef hit's planted right."

"Good fer ever' growin' thing. I mind—"

" 'Taint always. You got to know—"

"—when me and my wife wuz expectin' Eula," Uncle Billy continued, "One spring, 'twas. Already had two boys, we did, and I wanted some mo' gals. Raise a passel of boys, and they got to git out soon's they's wuth anything to a feller; got to set around and talk; but gals now: you kin keep 'em around the house and they'll work. So I hearn—"

"I mind, I wuz married in a April. Built my own house. They was a apple tree jest outside the winder. We used to lay there in the dark, a-watchin' it. Smellin' it, too."

"—that ef a woman laid in the moon, hit'd be a gal. So my wife taken and laid ever' night with the moon on her nekkid belly. I could lay my year onto hit and year Eula a-scrougin' inside her—"

"Whooey."

Mrs Littlejohn's house was dimensionless as cardboard. The veranda shadow gashed its face, and from the vague mellowness of the hall came Henry's voice Ah. Ah. Ah. Uncle Billy went on in, but the others stood quietly in the shadow near the door.

"Ther's one on the creek bridge," and they listened intently until the sound died away, and they moved one by one to the steps and sat down.

"Eck Snopes ought to've caught his'n when it run in the house yere."

"Looks like he ought."

The earth dreamed on, mysterious, rapturous, like a chord hushed, like an unborn chord held in suspension: the grave and tragic rythm of the world.

"Ther's that mockin'bird again."

Then Henry screamed again and they turned and looked at the vague door of the house, and presently Mrs Littlejohn came to the door. "Uncle Billy needs some help," she said.

"Whooey......" Clear and remote, reft by space of passion and indescribably sad, like the dying cadence of a bell: "Whooey...... goes......." Henry's scream consumed itself Ah. Ah. Ah. The mockingbird in the apple tree rippled tentatively, then swelled its throat and sang.

"Yes, sir—" V.K. Suratt finished his humorous recital amid their sober appreciative guffaws and grave spittings. They squatted in their faded earthy clothing on their heels against the weathered wall, or sat with their backs against the supporting posts of the veranda, engaged in trivial and intense occupations. With pocket knives, usually, trimming minutely at slivers of wood or whetting the worn blades on their shoes, pausing to spit with occasional and deliberate care, bending once more above their quiet slow hands. One held between his teeth a spray of peach with three blooms on it like miniature doll skirts of pink tulle and he took from his overalls a small tin and uncapped it and shook into the cap a measure of snuff and removed his peach spray and tilted his head and drew his lower lip away from his stained teeth. Suratt leaned among them against the wall, his bland affable face raptly benignant as he recapitulated with the studied effectiveness of the professional humorist. "Yes, sir, when I looked over my shoulder

63

and seen that thing in the do' behind me, a-blarin' hits eyes at me, I made sho' Flem Snopes had brung a tiger back from Texas with him."

I.O. Snopes, Flem's successor, sitting with his false merry eyes and his nutcracker face, tilted proprietorially in the single chair in the odorous broad door, slapped his thighs, cackling. "I reckon he'd a brung some ef he'd a knowed you fellers'd snap up them hosses so quick," he said. "Him and Buck'd a brung monkeys too, I reckon."

"And I reckon we'd a bought 'em," Suratt agreed sourly. The others sat in their slow sober preoccupations. "Say," Suratt asked, "How much did Flem make offen them hosses?"

"He made a plenty, I reckon," I.O. Snopes said. He cackled again, wisely: his mean little features clotted in the middle of his face like the plucking gesture of a hand. "Flem's putty cute, he is." The others sat in quiet absorption. One said, without raising his head:

"Flem claims he never had no interest in them hosses."

Suratt emitted a crude abrupt sound of disparagement. "Does anybody yere believe that?"

The man with the peach spray removed it and spat. "Will anybody yere ever know no better? Flem haint a-goin' to tell."

I.O. Snopes cackled again, with a kind of secretive glee. "Aint he a beatin' feller, now?" he said with frank admiration. "Yes, sir, Flem aint a-goin' to tell how much he made on them hosses."

"And you needn't to pretend like you knowed, neither," Suratt told I.O. Snopes. "Flem aint a-goin' to

tell you no quicker'n anybody else." I.O. Snopes continued to shake with niggard secretive mirth, rubbing
his palms on his thighs. "Yes, sir," Suratt continued
fretfully, "They wont nobody ever know how much he
made on them hosses, but I got my opinion of a feller
that'll bring a herd of wild cattymounts into a place
and sell 'em to his neighbors, and ef I was . . . ."
his voice ceased and they watched Flem Snopes quietly
as he came up the road whittling a bit of pine board and
mounted the steps. He greeted them generally and his
slow opaque eyes moved from one to another, and I.O.
Snopes rose with deference but deliberately and surren-
dered the chair and went to lean in the opposite side
of the door.

"I was jest a-tellin' Suratt," I.O. said, "that ef you'd
a knowed how these fellers'd snap up them hosses,
you'd a brung some monkeys and tigers back from
Texas, too."

Flem hooked his toes backward about the chair legs
and chewed with his slow thrusting detachment. "Buck
mought," he said briefly, and trimmed a sliver from
his stick. I.O. cackled again, with unction.

"Yes, sir," he repeated, "You boys cant git ahead of
Flem."

"Dont look like it," Suratt agreed. "Aint nobody ever
even caught up with him since last night. 'Cep' Henery
Armstid. And Vernon Turpin. Eck Snopes' hoss made
Vernon's mules run away on the bridge last night.
Snatched Vernon outen the waggin and skun him up
some. Vernon says he's a-goin' to law you fer it, Flem."

Flem chewed his steady tobacco and trimmed at
his stick with delicate preoccupation. The others

65

glanced at him covertly and quietly. Except Suratt. Suratt looked at Flem with a blend of curiosity and respect.

"Say, Flem," he said, and the others all listened without ostentation, "How much did you and that Texas feller make off of them hosses?"

"Better ask him," Flem answered. " 'Twarnt my hosses."

I.O. Snopes guffawed again, and V.K. Suratt joined him, but more temperately.

"Dont he beat 'em all," I.O. chortled. "Y'all might jes' well quit tryin' to git around Flem."

"That's right," Suratt agreed. "We all taken a back seat to Flem. Well, he sho' livened things up fer us, even if him and that Texas feller did skin us outen sixty or seventy dollars."

"How many'd you buy, V.K.?" he of the peach spray asked, and the others laughed with sober appreciation.

"I bought one less'n a lot of folks I know," Suratt rejoined. "Two less'n Eck Snopes yonder. I hearn fellers still after them hosses at ten o'clock last night. But Eck Snopes aint been home a-tall. Hi, Eck."

Eck and Admiral Dewey came without haste through the dust and mounted the veranda. "Hi, boys," Eck said generally and without inflection, and they responded with grave monosyllables, and Eck and Admiral Dewey crossed the veranda and I.O. Snopes followed them into the odorous dusty store.

"Yes, sir," Suratt continued, "even ol' Eck got trimmed. Not as bad as some, though: he was riskin' one fer two of 'em. Looks like a feller wouldn't trim his own blood kin, dont it, boys?" he added cunningly.

66

The others glanced covertly at Flem again, but he sat unmoved in his tilted chair, shaving with slow absorption at his pine stick.

Eck emerged again, with a paper sack, and he squatted against the wall and Admiral Dewey squatted in diminutive replica beside him, and he set the sack at his feet and took out his pocket knife and opened and stroked the blade on his thigh and took a segment of cheese from the sack and shaved off a piece and tendered it between the knife blade and his thumb. Admiral Dewey accepted it quietly, and Eck shaved off a piece for himself and took a handful of crackers from the paper bag and gave them to Admiral Dewey, and they squatted quietly against the wall and ate slowly and gravely and without selfconsciousness.

The man chewing the peach spray removed it and spat. "Say, Eck, how many of them things was they in Miz Littlejohn's house last night? V.K. Suratt says they was one in ever' room and you and her was chasin' two mo' up and down the hall with wash-boa'ds."

"'Twarnt but one," Eck answered, chewing. "Jest Ad's and mine."

"Well, hit was the biggest drove to have jest one hoss in it I ever seen in my life," Suratt said. "I'd a sworn they was a dozen, at least. Fer ten minutes, ever' time I looked behind or in front of me, there was that blare-eyed pink faced spotted thing jest runnin' over me er jest swirlin' to run over Eck Snopes. And that boy there, he stayed right under hit fer five minutes, I know."

They laughed again, with sober and indolent appreciation. Admiral Dewey with a bitten cracker in his small hand watched Suratt roundly with his grave periwinkle eyes, chewing steadily and without haste. The man with the peach spray removed it again.

"I wonder what that hoss thought Suratt was, a-jumpin' out winders and runnin' in do's in his shirt tail? I wonder how many Suratts that hoss thinks he seen?"

"I dont know," Suratt answered. "But if he seen half as many of me as I seen of him, he was sho' surrounded ever' way he jumped. Gentlemen, that hoss was in my room and on the front porch and I could year Mis' Littlejohn a-hittin' him with a wash-boa'd in the back yard, all at the same time. Still, he seemed to miss ever'body all right ever' time. I reckon that was what that feller meant by callin' them hosses bargains: I reckon he meant a feller'd have to be powerful unlucky to git clost enough to one of 'em to git hurt. Like Henery Armstid. Feller with a wife and fo' five chillen and not three pair o' shoes amongst 'em. Flem ought to be ashamed, sellin' him that hoss and lettin' him git his leg bruck, a-ketchin' hit. That was the last dollar Henery had in the world, I reckon, and him laid up in bed now, fixin' to lose a whole year, and his wife settin' up with him all night and he'pin' Miz Littlejohn all day fer Henery's and her keep. Yes, sir. Flem sho' ought to be ashamed," he repeated. The others sat gravely attentive. Flem chewed implacably, whittling at his stick.

(Page 23 of manuscript is missing)

Dewey his half and put his knife away. "Seen him run into hit after he met up with Vernon Turpin on the bridge. Knowed he couldn't git out, and he'd have to turn eround er jump a eight foot fence, so me and Ad taken and tied our rope acrosst the end of the lane. And putty soon, yere he come, hell-fer-leatherin' back down the lane wild as a mad dog and banged into that 'ere rope. He never seen it a-tall, I reckon.''

''Stopped 'im, did it?''

''Bruck his neck,'' Eck replied laconically. Admiral Dewey delved into the sack and exhumed a final cracker, which he ate slowly.

''What you goin' to do with 'im?'' I.O. Snopes asked with interest.

''Dunno yit,'' Eck answered. ''I already skun 'im. Dunno what I'll do with 'im yit.''

''Give 'im to me, paw,'' Admiral Dewey said.

''Which one was it?'' Flem asked. ''The one you bought, er the one Buck guv you?''

''The one he guv me,'' Eck answered. ''I never knowed which way the one I bought went.''

''Give 'im to me, paw,'' Admiral Dewey repeated. ''I holp to ketch 'im.''

''You kin have the other'n, ef you kin ketch 'im,'' his father said.

Jody Varner had called by Mrs Littlejohn's to inquire after Henry Armstid, and from there he took a short cut across Mrs Littlejohn's back yard and entered his store from the rear, where he paused in midstride like a bird dog pointing. Then he moved again, with astonishing secrecy for one of his flourishing bulk, and through the near obscurity he stole swiftly and passed behind the counter and sped on and savagely exhumed a hulking half grown boy from the glass case where he

69

kept his gaudy candy.

The boy emitted a choked sound of astonishment and alarm, and struggled. But he stopped almost at once, and became slack in Jody's grasp and Jody dragged him unresisting around the counter as I.O. Snopes entered. Those sitting and squatting on the veranda craned their necks quietly. "You, Cla'ence," I.O. Snopes said.

"Aint I tole you and tole you to keep this dam' boy outen yere?" Jody said, shaking his lax captive. "He's dang near et that candy case clean. Stan' up!" The boy stood, chewing, with a kind of static fatalism, without looking at anything exactly. "Look at that 'ere candy case!" Jody repeated. "Nigh cleaned out. Next thing I know, he'll graze on back ther' and work through that lace leather and them ringbolts and eat me and you and him right on out the back do'." Jody released him. "Stan' up, boy!"

"Git on home, Cla'ence," I.O. said, and the boy moved toward the back door.

"Yere," Jody said. "This way," and jerked his head toward the front entrance, and the boy obeyed. "And if I ketch him hangin' around yere again, I'm a-goin' to set a bear trap fer him."

The boy crossed the veranda, and Admiral Dewey watched him quietly, and descended the steps and went on up the road. His scanty overalls undulated tightly across his slow flabby thighs, and he put his hand into his pocket and then lifted it to his mouth.

Jody Varner came to the door. "Morning, gentlemen," he said, breathing heavily, and sawed at a plug of tobacco with his knife and thrust a piece into his mouth. "Year you caught one o' yer hosses, Eck."

III

Twilight in these latitudes, in late April, accomplishes itself promptly. Not suddenly, yet without any Yankee reluctance. You walk through the dust toward Mrs Littlejohn's imminent supper bell; there is no longer any sun on the dust and it is of a simple tone and unemphatic as shallow water about your shoe soles, but there is yet a mellow slant of it like a ruined column of Dorian marble across the ridged hills beyond Jody Varner's store, and in the apple tree opposite Mrs Littlejohn's veranda a sourceless and tattered scrap of it is caught like a lady's hasty and anonymous veil. The recurrent virginity of the apple tree, mid-moons couched between by lusty embrace of the year, has doffed its blooms; in the adjacent barnyard the sparrows are still garrulous in a final chorus, like refugees alarmed and sibilant above the mounting tide of violet shadows; about chimneys swallows yet in erratic indecision.

But supper over, you emerged into a different world. A world of lilac peace, in which Varner's store and the blacksmith shop were like sunken derelicts in the motionless and forgotten caverns of the sea. No sound, no movement; no tide to knock their sleeping bones together. And yet it was not quite night. The west was green and tall and without depth, like a pane of glass; through it a substance that was not light seeped in sourceless diffusion, like the sound of an organ.

Suratt's buckboard stood at the hitching rail.

III

Facsimile section of William Faulkner's manuscript of *Father Abraham*